grade

2

CW00327746

For full details of exam requir
current syllabus in conjun
Information & Regulations and
teachers and parents, *These*
documents are available onli............abrsm.org, as
well as free of charge from music retailers, from ABRSM
local representatives or from the Services Department,
The Associated Board of the Royal Schools of Music,
24 Portland Place, London W1B 1LU, United Kingdom.

CONTENTS AND TRACK LISTING

In this album, editorial additions to the texts are given in small print, within square brackets, or – in the case of slurs and ties – in the form ⌢. Metronome marks, breath marks (retained here where they appear in the source edition) and ornament realizations (suggested for exam purposes) are for guidance only; they are not comprehensive or obligatory.

Footnotes: Anthony Burton

**DO NOT
PHOTOCOPY
© MUSIC**

Alternative pieces for this grade

Music origination by Barnes Music Engraving Ltd
Cover by Økvik Design
Printed in England by Halstan & Co. Ltd, Amersham, Bucks.

Minuet

Edited by
Trevor Wye

BLAVET

Michel Blavet (1700–68), although self-taught (he actually played left-handed, which was possible on the one-keyed flute of the time), became the leading flautist in Paris and the most famous exponent of his instrument in the whole of Europe. His compositions include three sets of sonatas and many shorter pieces for flute and continuo – that is, a bass line with indications of the harmonies to be filled in by the keyboard player in the right hand (the right-hand part here is editorial).

AB 3340

Marche militaire

D. 733 No. 1

A:2

Arranged by
Ian Denley

SCHUBERT

Franz Schubert (1797–1828) was the last of the great composers of what is called the Viennese classical period, though his music also looks forward to the Romanticism of the later 19th century. This is a shortened and simplified arrangement of the first section of a well-known 'Military March' for piano duet (four hands at one keyboard), the first of a set of three which he wrote in 1818. *Alla marcia* simply means 'in march time'; Schubert's original marking was *Allegro vivace*.

AB 3340

Menuet

Second movement from *Hochzeit-Divertissement*

TELEMANN

Edited and continuo realization by
Winfried Michel

Georg Philipp Telemann (1681–1767) was a German contemporary and friend of Bach and Handel, at least as famous as either at the time, and a prolific composer of every kind of music. This Menuet comes from a 'Musikalisch-Choréographisches Hochzeit-Divertissement', a wedding entertainment in music and dancing, published in Frankfurt around 1718. The piece is laid out for a treble instrument or voice (there were originally words as well) and continuo, with the right-hand keyboard part to be improvised by the player (the one here is by the editor). The dynamics are suggestions for exam purposes and may be varied. The repeats should not be played in the exam; however, in other performances a few more ornaments could be added on the repeats.

Hungarian Fantaisie

Op. 2

Edited by
Sally Adams and Nigel Morley

J. ANDERSEN

B:1

The Danish flautist Joachim Andersen (1847–1909) was a founder-member of the Berlin Philharmonic Orchestra in 1881, and was also a conductor and a composer of flute pieces and studies. This *Hungarian Fantaisie* is in the gypsy style made popular by the Hungarian Dances of Brahms; in this style, the tempo may be treated with some freedom, and dotted rhythms and short rests slightly exaggerated, to create a strutting, swaggering effect.

Reproduced from *First Repertoire for Flute* by permission of the publishers. All enquiries about this piece, apart from those directly relating to the exams, should be addressed to Faber Music Ltd, 3 Queen Square, London WC1N 3AU.

B:2

Naughty, but Nice!

No. 3 from *Easy Jazzy Flute*

JAMES RAE

James Rae was born in 1957 on Tyneside, studied at the Guildhall School of Music & Drama, and is now a saxophonist, teacher and composer specializing in educational wind music. This piece, from a collection published in 1995, has a regular rhythm in the left hand of the piano which is associated both with the Argentinean tango and with the Cuban habanera.

AB 3340

The Liberty Bell

B:3

Arranged by
Ian Denley

J. P. SOUSA

John Philip Sousa (1854–1932) was famous as the conductor of the US Marine Band and later of his own touring band, and as the composer of well over a hundred quick marches, all with an irresistible spring in their step. His 1893 march *The Liberty Bell*, of which this is a shortened version, is named after the famous bell in Philadelphia which in 1776 summoned citizens to the reading of the American Declaration of Independence. The piece was well known long before it was adopted in 1969 for the television comedy series *Monty Python's Flying Circus*, in a rudely truncated form.

Reproduced from *Flute Time 1* by permission. All enquiries about this piece, apart from those directly relating to the exams, should be addressed to Oxford University Press, Music Department, Great Clarendon Street, Oxford OX2 6DP.

Study in G

No. 18 from *First Exercises for Flute*

GARIBOLDI

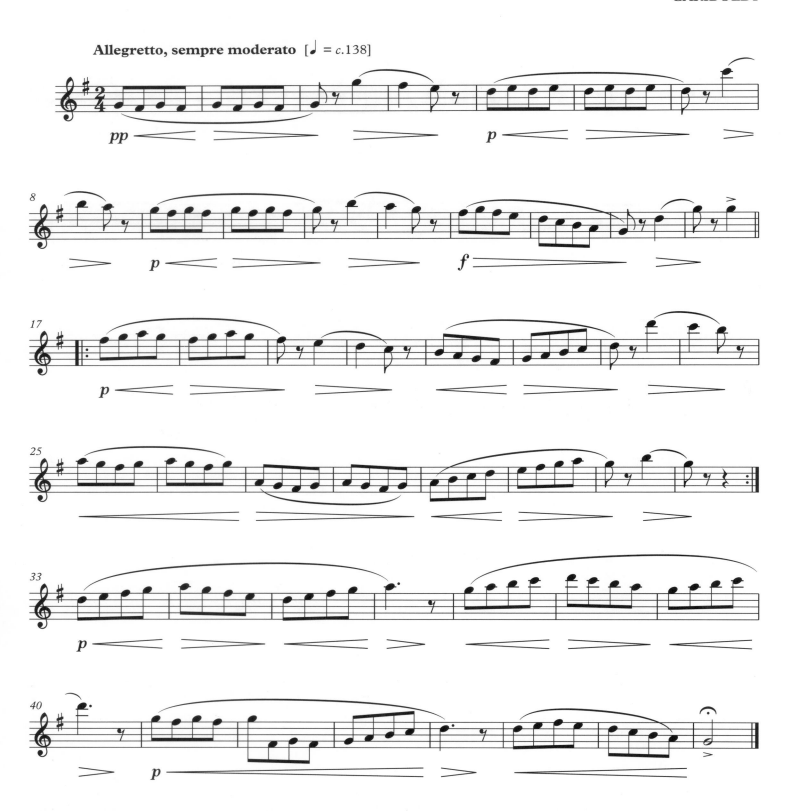

Giuseppe Gariboldi (1833–1905) was an Italian flautist who worked for many years in Paris; his publications, which amounted to several hundred, included numerous compositions, arrangements and studies for the flute. This study, from a collection for beginners, requires even fingerwork and careful observance of the dynamic markings.

Humoreske

from *A Miscellany for Flute*, Book I

C:2

MICHAEL ROSE

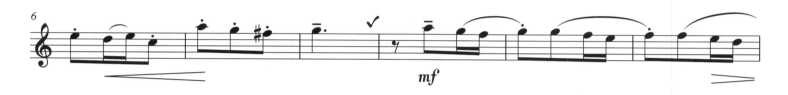

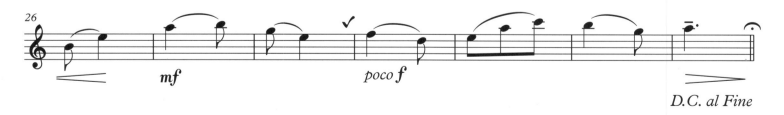

D.C. al Fine

The English composer, conductor and teacher Michael Rose (b. 1934) has extensive experience of music in education and has written much music for young players. This piece, not so much 'humorous' as 'good-humoured', is from a collection published in 1991. It is in the rhythm (one beat to a bar) of the 18th-century dance called the passepied, and it has an 18th-century form with a middle section, or 'trio', followed by an exact reprise of the main section. Make the most of the contrast between the bright, spiky outer sections and the much smoother trio.

Study in Purple

from *Fresh Air for Flute*

SARAH WATTS

Sarah Watts studied at the Royal College of Music and now spends much of her time composing, her output ranging from classroom tutor books to musicals and choral works. She is also Artistic Director of the National Youth Music Camps. This piece is one of a series of studies with different colour names, from a collection published in 2005. To help you keep the pulse going steadily through the rests, imagine a bass player plucking four steady beats to the bar.

grade 2 Flute exam pieces

Piano accompaniment

For full details of exam requirements, please refer to the current syllabus in conjunction with *Examination Information & Regulations* and the guide for candidates, teachers and parents, *These Music Exams*. These three documents are available online at www.abrsm.org, as well as free of charge from music retailers, from ABRSM local representatives or from the Services Department, The Associated Board of the Royal Schools of Music, 24 Portland Place, London W1B 1LU, United Kingdom.

REQUIREMENTS

SCALES AND ARPEGGIOS (from memory, to be played both slurred and tongued)

F, G majors; E, A minors (one octave)
D major (two octaves)

Scales
in the above keys (minors in melodic *or* harmonic form at candidate's choice)

Arpeggios
the common chords of the above keys for the ranges indicated

PLAYING AT SIGHT (see current syllabus)

AURAL TESTS (see current syllabus)

THREE PIECES   *page*

Candidates must prepare three pieces, one from each of the three Lists, A, B and C. Candidates may choose from the pieces printed in this album or any other piece listed for the grade. A full list is given in the current syllabus.

Footnotes: Anthony Burton

© 2007 by The Associated Board of the Royal Schools of Music

No part of this publication may be copied or reproduced in any form or by any means without the prior permission of the publisher.

Music origination by Barnes Music Engraving Ltd

Cover by Økvik Design

Printed in England by Halstan & Co. Ltd, Amersham, Bucks.

In this album, editorial additions to the texts are given in small print, within square brackets, or – in the case of slurs and ties – in the form ⌢. Metronome marks, breath marks (retained here where they appear in the source edition) and ornament realizations (suggested for exam purposes) are for guidance only; they are not comprehensive or obligatory.

Minuet

Edited by
Trevor Wye

BLAVET

Michel Blavet (1700–68), although self-taught (he actually played left-handed, which was possible on the one-keyed flute of the time), became the leading flautist in Paris and the most famous exponent of his instrument in the whole of Europe. His compositions include three sets of sonatas and many shorter pieces for flute and continuo – that is, a bass line with indications of the harmonies to be filled in by the keyboard player in the right hand (the right-hand part here is editorial).

Marche militaire

D. 733 No. 1

Arranged by
Ian Denley

SCHUBERT

Franz Schubert (1797–1828) was the last of the great composers of what is called the Viennese classical period, though his music also looks forward to the Romanticism of the later 19th century. This is a shortened and simplified arrangement of the first section of a well-known 'Military March' for piano duet (four hands at one keyboard), the first of a set of three which he wrote in 1818. *Alla marcia* simply means 'in march time'; Schubert's original marking was *Allegro vivace*.

Menuet

Second movement from *Hochzeit-Divertissement*

Edited and continuo realization by
Winfried Michel

TELEMANN

DO NOT
PHOTOCOPY
© MUSIC

Georg Philipp Telemann (1681–1767) was a German contemporary and friend of Bach and Handel, at least as famous as either at the time, and a prolific composer of every kind of music. This Menuet comes from a 'Musikalisch-Choréographisches Hochzeit-Divertissement', a wedding entertainment in music and dancing, published in Frankfurt around 1718. The piece is laid out for a treble instrument or voice (there were originally words as well) and continuo, with the right-hand keyboard part to be improvised by the player (the one here is by the editor). The dynamics are suggestions for exam purposes and may be varied. The repeats should not be played in the exam; however, in other performances a few more ornaments could be added on the repeats.

Hungarian Fantaisie

Op. 2

Edited by
Sally Adams and Nigel Morley

B:1

J. ANDERSEN

The Danish flautist Joachim Andersen (1847–1909) was a founder-member of the Berlin Philharmonic Orchestra in 1881, and was also a conductor and a composer of flute pieces and studies. This *Hungarian Fantaisie* is in the gypsy style made popular by the Hungarian Dances of Brahms; in this style, the tempo may be treated with some freedom, and dotted rhythms and short rests slightly exaggerated, to create a strutting, swaggering effect.

Naughty, but Nice!

No. 3 from *Easy Jazzy Flute*

JAMES RAE

James Rae was born in 1957 on Tyneside, studied at the Guildhall School of Music & Drama, and is now a saxophonist, teacher and composer specializing in educational wind music. This piece, from a collection published in 1995, has a regular rhythm in the left hand of the piano which is associated both with the Argentinean tango and with the Cuban habanera.

CODA

D.S. al Coda

B:3

The Liberty Bell

Arranged by
Ian Denley

J. P. SOUSA

John Philip Sousa (1854–1932) was famous as the conductor of the US Marine Band and later of his own touring band, and as the composer of well over a hundred quick marches, all with an irresistible spring in their step. His 1893 march *The Liberty Bell*, of which this is a shortened version, is named after the famous bell in Philadelphia which in 1776 summoned citizens to the reading of the American Declaration of Independence. The piece was well known long before it was adopted in 1969 for the television comedy series *Monty Python's Flying Circus*, in a rudely truncated form.

Reproduced from *Flute Time 1* by permission. All enquiries about this piece, apart from those directly relating to the exams, should be addressed to Oxford University Press, Music Department, Great Clarendon Street, Oxford OX2 6DP.